Other books by A. K. Yearling

Daring Do and the Quest for the Sapphire Stone

Daring Do and the Griffon's Goblet

Daring Do and the Abyss of Despair

Daring Do and the Razor of Dreams

Daring Do and the Ring of Destiny

Daring Do and the Trek to the Terrifying Tower

Daring Do and the Volcano of Destiny

Daring Do and the Marked Thief of Marapore

Daring Do and the Eternal Flower

Daring Do and the Forbidden City of Clouds

Other books by G. M. Berrow

Twilight Sparkle and the Crystal Heart Spell

Pinkie Pie and the Rockin' Ponypalooza Party!

Rainbow Dash and the Daring Do Double Dare

Rarity and the Curious Case of Charity

Applejack and the Honest-to-Goodness Switcheroo

DARING DO and the ETERNAL FLOWER

By A. K. Yearling
with G. M. Berrow

Little, Brown and Company
New York Boston

Cover illustration by Franco Spagnolo

Little, Brown and Company

Hachette Book Group
1290 Avenue of the Americas, New York, NY 10104
Visit us at lb-kids.com

Little, Brown and Company is a division of Hachette Book Group, Inc. The Little, Brown name and logo are trademarks of Hachette Book Group, Inc.

First Stand-Alone Edition: April 2016
Originally published as part of *My Little Pony: The Daring Do Adventure Collection* in October 2014 by Little, Brown and Company

Library of Congress Control Number: 2014940995

ISBN 978-0-316-38934-1

10 9 8 7 6 5 4 3 2 1

RRD-C

Printed in the United States of America

For Erin, to whom I am
eternally grateful

TABLE OF CONTENTS

CHAPTER 1
The Grandest Affair in the Land 1

CHAPTER 2
Daring Takes the Lead 19

CHAPTER 3
The Reading Room of the
Equestrian Botanical Society 33

CHAPTER 4
The Key to Gallant True 43

CHAPTER 5
The Diary and the Everleaf 57

CHAPTER 6
To Catch a Leaf Thief 65

CHAPTER 7
A Fortress on the Edge of the World 83

CHAPTER 8
The Ambush of Ahuizotl 101

CHAPTER 9
The Secret of the Everleaves 111

CHAPTER 10
Travel the Scales 125

CHAPTER 11
An Oasis of Fire and Flowers 143

CHAPTER 12
Indigenous Plants
and Ingenious Plans 151

CHAPTER 13
Tears of the Dragon 161

CHAPTER 14
Grotto of the Moon 167

CHAPTER 15
The Infinity Root 175

CHAPTER 16
The Treasure 187

CHAPTER 1

The Grandest Affair in the Land

There were a hundred lively conversations taking place at once in the grand ballroom, but only one mattered to Daring Do. She wasn't a part of it…yet. But she would be, as soon as she could make her move toward the board of directors. Daring didn't want this entire night to have been for nothing. The fancy mane updo, the uncomfortably snug sequined ball gown, and the absolute agony of having to socialize for hours with ponies she knew nothing about (nor cared about, for that matter) were all means to an end.

Tonight was the night Daring Do would find out the truth about the Eternal Flower and if it was really able to grant a pony the unfathomable legendary prize—immortality. For all she knew, it was a myth like so many other leads throughout her career had been. But Daring Do had a strong feeling about this one, and it would not be silenced.

The evening was a posh event. There were fifty massive round tables. Each was covered in a crisp white tablecloth and set for ten guests. Gorgeous blooms of

jasmine, lavender, and rainbow hibiscus were arranged into tall centerpieces, and they filled the air with perfumed fresh-ness, delighting everypony. Each lucky guest's place was set with gold-plated utensils, fresh flower petals, and an exclu-sive party favor. There was a tiny chocolate truffle in the shape of a rose, and next to it was a real long-stemmed blossom with a card bearing the guest's name.

MS. DARING DO—HONORED GUEST OF THE EQUESTRIAN BOTANICAL SOCIETY. The elab-orate calligraphy bore many loops and swirls, much like the vines of ivy that cov-ered the bandstand. Twinkling white fairy lights were draped throughout, cascading down from the ceiling like the branches of a weeping willow tree. Society ponies,

the ones who always attended these benefits, loved the intricate details. They'd buy an expensive ticket, get dressed up in their finery, and dance the night away, all in the name of some cause or another. Any excuse for a party.

A young mare wearing diamond-encrusted hoofcuffs trotted past Daring's table. "What's the cause of the evening again?" she asked her friend, who was checking her bright blue eye shadow in a small pocket mirror.

"Something to do with saving flowers," the friend replied. "I just love flowers, don't you?" she added before the pair cantered off to apply more makeup and make more vague yet supportive statements about the event of the evening.

Bubbles fizzed on Daring's tongue as she took a delicate sip from her flute of sparkling cider. The mare pretended to listen to General Sparks prattle on about his collection of rare Horavian bits, but she was actually too preoccupied with scanning the room to bother with numismatics. The sea of taffeta, tulle, and tuxedos was a hindrance to her goal: find the scholars who knew something about her current obsession.

According to the only botanical journal of the society Flora and Foalna, she should be looking for two specific society members named Vine and Fern, who had published a recent article entitled "Reaching into Eternity: The Legend of the Eternal Flower." Daring had wisely taken the extra time to secure a copy of the guest list before the event, so she knew they would be there.

"Oh, what the hay!" Sparks chuckled in amusement. "How about some visuals, too, so you can really get a sense of what I'm describing?" The general pulled out his wallet, flipping through the photos one by one. "Ah yes! Here is one of my favorites…the magnificent Morrow Era silver two-bit piece, circa 796 Before Celestia…" He adjusted his monocle and smiled at Daring. "Isn't it a beauty?" His curled white mustache moved with each word he spoke.

"Wow, never seen anything like it…" the adventurer replied with a courteous nod and a forced smile. Daring's attention was not on the pony in front of her. Where were those two ponies with the secret information she was desperate to obtain? The only reason she was in attendance at this ridiculously over-the-top fund-raiser for the Equestrian Botanical Society was to spy on them.

Over by the dessert table, Daring spotted a light gray pony with a dark purple mane chatting with a stallion who *could* have been a scholar. But the guy wouldn't turn around.

"Would you care for another glass of cider, miss?" A white-gloved waiter appeared, wearing a black jacket and bow tie, bottle in hoof.

"Yes," Daring snapped, and craned her neck around him. "But hurry." She wouldn't have minded if he weren't blocking her entire view of the room. The waiter topped her off and stepped over to the next guest. If Daring was going to have to stay for the entire event of speeches and presentations, she might as well sip some of the sweet bubbly concoction.

Suddenly, she spotted the duo. Her targets were all the way on the opposite side of the grand space, at another table, completely out of earshot. But Daring Do was a master lip-reader. She smoothed down a few wisps of her gray-and-black mane, which was done up in an incredibly uncomfortable French twist. The pony was the picture of sophisticated elegance in her shimmering olive-green ball gown. Daring hated nothing more than dressing up, but as long as she looked at it as another one of her expert disguises, she could deal with being a bit fillyish for one night. Seeing her reflection in the mirror was still odd, however.

The band switched to a fast number, and several ponies got up to take part in the merriment. The guests began pairing off, twirling and stomping their hooves to the beat.

"Excuse me for my ill manners, Miss Do. I would ask you to dance, but I'm afraid I have four left hooves." Sparks bowed his head to her, his monocle almost falling off his left eye. He'd taken the hint and stashed his pictures back in his coat pocket. "Though if you begged, I could attempt a fox-trot...."

Daring Do waved her hoof and shook her head in response. "That's quite all right, General. I *don't* dance. Actually, I—"

Daring cut herself off midsentence. She took another gulp of cider and watched with focused intent on an ancient little mare wearing a high-necked, ruffled black ball gown chatting with a rotund young stallion in a brown suit. Madame Willow Fern and Mr. Thaddeus Vine, respectively. Not only were they members of the board and experts on every type of grass, tree, and flower known to ponykind, but they also had theories on the specific item she was interested in. If anypony would have the information she was searching for— the actual truth of the Eternal Flower—it was the two of them.

Their eyes shifted around as they spoke, clearly suspicious that they were being listened to. "—after the presentation we'll take her—" Madame Fern was saying. Her painted red lips were a bright contrast to her teal-colored hide and emphasized each word.

"Maybe we should do it now while—" Mr. Vine frowned. His bushy yellow mustache made it more difficult to read his lips. He looked over his shoulder at the crowd of ponies rushing the fresh batch of caramel apple tarts. "Nopony will notice if she's missing—"

Ponies crossed in front of Daring, heading to the dance floor, unknowingly causing her to miss words here and there. But she didn't dare to move now.

"—might not believe—" Vine said.

More ponies crossed through Daring's line of vision. *Get out of the way!* thought Daring.

Vine was still talking. "—dire circumstances!"

"—then she will go, that's what he said—"

Two mares paused in front of their table, fixing each other's mane updos before continuing on toward the cider station. Maybe it was time to lurk a bit closer.

"—location of the Eternal Flower!" Fern exclaimed, her face riddled with concern.

Vine gasped and put his hoof over Fern's mouth. "Not here."

Daring leaned forward, her eyes growing wide. Her instincts had been correct! They *did* know something about the item Daring Do sought.

There were many reasons to believe the mythical bloom was indeed real. For the most part, Daring Do only hunted for items that were more tangible, or at least made of something sturdy like gold or Earth pony steel. Flowers were alive and, in turn, ephemeral—a pony could quest a whole lifetime for a rare plant, only to find that the species had become extinct. Daring Do didn't like to set herself up for disappointment. Tangible objects that lasted forever were her game.

But after the recent events in Marapore, where Daring had rescued the villagers from the fiery eruption of Mount Vehoovius, her opinions had changed on the matter. Golden Rule, the local Maraporean scholar, had given her a parting gift: *Indigenous Magical Plants of the North and South, Volume 5: Flowers.* The rare book contained a wealth of information on the subject, including a cryptic entry on the Eternal Flower: the only plant that was believed to last forever.

The elusive magical blossom was understood to be the giver of immortality to anypony who consumed its sweet nectar. The only trouble was that nopony knew where to find it. Even if they did, they would never be able to pass along the information, since the bloom replanted itself in a new location each time it was seen. To make matters even more complicated, it was said that the flower evolved each time by developing new attributes based on whoever was looking for it. The Eternal Flower did not want to be found. So, naturally, Daring Do had to have it.

The song ended and a new one began. It was a slow tune.

Enough waiting and plotting from across the room! Daring stood up and trotted straight to Madame and Thaddeus's table, leaving the general open-mouthed at her hasty departure. Daring reached out her hoof to the startled Thaddeus Vine and raised her eyebrows. "Care to dance, Mr. Vine?"

The poor stallion was barely able to mutter a response before Daring Do was tackled to the floor by two strong hench-ponies in tuxedos. Daring had made a rookie mistake. She had been so busy watching her own targets all evening that she hadn't bothered to notice she was a target, too—of Dr. Caballeron himself!

CHAPTER 2
Daring Takes the Lead

The sleeve of the sequined dress tore as Daring Do sprang to her hooves, shoving the heavy ponies off her. She couldn't care less if the frock was ruined. The gauzy swathes of olive fabric made every movement twice as difficult. With a graceful pirouette, Daring spun on her back hoof and pummeled the two burly ponies, sending them sliding across the slick wooden dance floor. The bigger of the two, a pony with a short orange mane, slammed against one of the tables. He grunted in defeat, and the floral centerpiece crashed to the ground, shards of silver glass exploding everywhere. The ponies seated at the table gasped in shock at the scene, shielding their precious faces. A few of the mares cried out, though it was unclear if they were upset about the fight or the spilled cider on their dresses.

The room began to empty out. The band played on, switching the song to an upbeat number that matched the action unfolding in front of them.

"Anypony else want to tango?" Daring Do called out to the two henchponies she

could see. The ponies, disguised as wait-
ers, looked to one another with blank
expressions. They weren't the most intelli-
gent of characters. "No? Well, I guess that
means I'm doing a solo performance!"
Daring spread her wings and soared up
to the twelve-tiered Crystal Empire chandelier. She flew at top speed, encircling
the massive fixture in a dizzying tornado
of gold, gray, and glittering green. The
crystals on the chandelier shone through
the blur and appeared as a mesmeriz-
ing light show. Everypony down below
stopped in their tracks, including the
waiter henchponies. The band picked up
the pace to add to the excitement. Daring
pushed to go even faster. One of her favorite tricks to defeat an enemy was to create

a confusing distraction. Worked every time.

"It's going to fall!" a Pegasus mare in a yellow gown cried out. Her face twisted in horror as she motioned to the swaying chandelier. The supports on one side had snapped, and now only a single steel chain suspended it. "Everypony, run!"

Ponies scrambled to the edges of the room, but the two waiter henchponies stood their ground. The other two were still groaning on the floor, holding their heads. Daring Do peeled off toward the corner, where the ceiling met the top of the wall. The gigantic chandelier circled like a pendulum with momentum. Exactly as Daring calculated it would. She bit her lip in anticipation. It would just be a second until...

WHAM!

As the chandelier dropped down, it landed on a table with a loud crash, demolishing everything except the table itself. Pieces of crystal dislodged and shattered like shining fireworks. Then the table rolled onto its side and careened toward another, creating a domino effect that resulted in five tables creating a barrier around the four henchponies in the middle of the dance floor. They were trapped!

"I call that one the box step!" Daring laughed from above. Catching the group of ponies had been relatively easy. Just a quick dash, a swoop, and a crash, and now they were completely helpless. Dr. Caballeron always hired such oafs to work for him, but it made her job easier. Brute strength was nothing against cunning wit and agility. Even in a formal evening gown.

"Not so fast, Do!" a familiar voice rang out across the cavernous ballroom. It had a distinctly foreign lilt. Daring Do would know that voice anywhere.

"Caballeron!" Daring growled, searching the crowd. She furrowed her brow and zeroed in on him, standing by the very table she was trying to approach when the scuffle broke out. It was where the board of directors of the Equestrian Botanical Society was sitting. "Haven't you learned to mind your own business by now?" she taunted him.

The smarmy stallion smirked and smoothed back his short salt-and-pepper mane. The stubble on his chin was overgrown, like he'd been on the road for weeks. And judging by his outfit—the usual tan shirt and red polka-dot scarf—Caballeron hadn't been attending the event. He had been waiting in the wings for his moment to swoop in and ruin everything for everypony.

Caballeron paced back and forth, his cutie mark of a gold skull with red and white gems in its eyes moving almost as if it were talking. "On the contrary, Do. I have kept a closer watch on you than ever...." He trotted over to Fern and Vine. Rope was already bound around their hooves, and tape had been placed across their muzzles. They squirmed and cried out, but their pleas were undecipherable. Madame Willow Fern looked like she was about to faint. "And my new friends Willow and Thaddeus here have agreed to help make you cooperate with my requests." He touched the madame's chin with his hoof and winked. She squirmed, her face contorted into an expression of anguish. "Isn't that right, my lovely madame?"

"Release them, Caballeron!" Daring shouted. "You have no quarrel with the members of the board. This is between you...and *me*." She flew over and landed on a nearby table, her head positioned down and teeth exposed in a tight clench. Her eyes narrowed. There was no way Dr. Caballeron was going to ruin any more of this night. The remaining guests were gathered together in little groups, tittering about the lack of security at the affair and wondering if they could get their bits refunded. Typical high-society ponies in a crisis—worried about small things instead of their own safety.

"I'll release them on one condition, Daring Do...." Caballeron sauntered up to her. "You let me and my ponies walk away free right now." He raised a brow. "Deal?"

"What's the catch?" Daring jumped off the table and met him eye-to-eye. Caballeron had a sneaky look on his face. It could only mean one thing. "You're up to something, and I don't like it." She raised a suspicious brow, searching his face for hidden clues.

"Let's just say we got what we came for." Dr. Caballeron sneered. "And that the Eternal Flower will be found!" The pony held up a clear glass bottle, inspecting it with satisfaction. Inside was a single leaf, the edges a dark jade color fading into a vibrant lime toward the stem. Tiny gold specks sprayed across it like freckles across a muzzle. The fact that Dr. Caballeron wanted it so badly meant it must be valuable. Caballeron smiled, his eyes alight with victory. "Ahuizotl is going to be so delighted when we hoof-deliver this specimen to him."

"Hawking stolen goods for money again, Caballeron?" Daring scoffed. "I would expect nothing else from you."

Suddenly, Mr. Vine locked eyes with Daring. He gave her a tiny nod that seemed to say, *Let him go.* Message received—the bottle with the leaf was of no consequence to Vine. The transaction was so subtle that Caballeron missed it entirely.

"Just scram, Caballeron!" Daring growled through gritted teeth. "And don't let me catch you coming anywhere near Madame Willow Fern or Mr. Thaddeus Vine again."

"Excellent choice, my dear." Dr. Caballeron smirked, stepping away from his hostages. He trotted over to the enclosure where his henchponies were trapped and bucked his hind legs against one of the tables. The heavy table budged enough for the ponies to escape. They came spilling out, their suits rumpled and creased, and their expressions sheepish. It was not the first time Daring Do had defeated them without so much as batting an eyelash.

As the band of ruffians gathered themselves, Daring took the opportunity to untie Vine and Fern. The rope had burned their hooves and wrinkled their fancy clothes.

"Adios, Daring Do!" Dr. Caballeron called out as he hoofed it over to the main entrance archway. He stopped for a moment and turned around, a sly look on his face. "By the way, Daring, you really should consider wearing dresses more often. You look kind of…nice." Then he and his ponies turned on their hooves and cantered out the door and into the dark night. Daring Do had never been more irate. *Nopony* told her she looked *nice*.

CHAPTER 3
The Reading Room of the Equestrian Botanical Society

Madame Willow Fern's once-beautiful black ruffled gown was stained from where an apple tart had toppled onto her lap, and her mascara was running down her cheeks. Her graying mane was falling out of its braided updo. The little pins stuck out every which way, and as she trotted, one would occasionally fall onto the wooden hallway floor with a tiny *click*. Yet there was a determination in her eyes as she led Daring Do and Mr. Thaddeus Vine through the hallways of the Equestrian Botanical Society.

Due to her advanced age, the mare couldn't trot as fast as her counterparts. They tried their best to remain calm and patient despite the urgency of the situation. Daring gave Vine the side-eye, and he snapped to action. "Do you, uh... need a hoof, Willow?" The mare promptly brushed him off with an unceremonious grunt.

Things couldn't get much worse for Daring's new acquaintances. In one fell swoop, Dr. Caballeron had managed to ruin the entire Equestrian Botanical Society banquet with his ambush. On top of that, the wicked stallion had gotten away with stealing a precious rare leaf. Daring couldn't help but wonder what made the plant so special, but her gut told her not to mention it until they got to the board members' library. It was the safest place in the building, according to Madame. A bunker in disguise—soundproof and impenetrable to unwanted intruders. *Perhaps they should have left the leaf specimen in there*, Daring thought as she trudged after the pair.

The timeworn building reminded Daring Do of her university days, which were spent roaming the dark, wood-paneled halls of academia, soaking up every piece of information like a sponge. Instead of likenesses of famous archaeologists, these walls were adorned with paintings of famous botanists and the plants they'd discovered. The air smelled stale and dusty with an undertone of fresh flowers, thanks to the beautiful arrangements on each of the credenzas. Daring counted at least twenty doors before they finally reached the one that said READING ROOM.

"It's just in here, dear." Madame Fern glanced back at Daring and shook her head. "I knew we should have found you first."

"After you." Mr. Vine bowed his head, eyes downcast in a mournful manner. Daring wondered if the stolen leaf in the jar had belonged to him. Perhaps it was part of some research and he had been on the verge of a scientific breakthrough.

Once inside, the air became thick, and Daring could almost hear the silence. The shelves upon shelves of dusty old books were great for absorbing noise, making it a perfect room for a top secret meeting.

Daring Do planted her flank on the edge of a brown leather sofa and got straight to business. "So, what were you two talking about before Caballeron decided to drop in?"

The two scholars exchanged a worried look. "Go on, Willow." Vine nodded toward the old mare. "It's okay. Tell her everything."

"There isn't much time, so I'll be concise—Caballeron has taken the Eternal

Leaf." She sat down in the armchair across from Daring and riffled through her jeweled clutch. "The whole point of this evening, my dear, was to recruit you for a mission."

"A mission?" Daring raised an eyebrow. Madame Fern had her full attention now. "Of what nature?"

Willow waved a hoof. "Well, I suppose it was *originally* a quest but has now turned into a rescue mission." She shook her head in regret. "I just wish—"

"We need you to find somepony." Vine cut her off as he reached into the pocket of his purple waistcoat and pulled out a mahogany pipe. He lit it, took a long draw, and exhaled a cloud of smoke. "Our trusty colleague Gallant True is missing."

He pointed to an oil painting on the wall. The Unicorn stallion pictured was smiling—goofy yet noble. His thinning, short mane was dusty yellow, with a neat, trimmed mustache to match. It was nothing like Thaddeus Vine's, which Daring thought looked distinctly like two large caterpillars had decided to nestle atop his muzzle. The pony in the portrait had a coat the color of milk chocolate, wire-framed glasses, and a navy-blue bow tie.

"That's him...?" Daring felt her heart beat faster. "*That's* Gallant True?"

Vine nodded, looking at the portrait wistfully. "Poor fellow was one of our top researchers, but he had taken the Eternal Flower project all on his own. It was he who'd hoped to bring you here tonight and recruit you to go out and find it with him…."

Daring Do stood up and walked closer to the painting. It was definitely him. The missing pony was none other than her own uncle.

CHAPTER 4
The Key to Gallant True

The face staring back at her from the painting was such a sight for sore eyes. Daring Do had known the pony by another name—he was her uncle Adventure. When she was just a little filly, Uncle Ad would come to stay for weeks at a time. The brawny Unicorn would spend his days writing research papers and creating fake quests for his niece. They had been the highlights of her childhood.

There were treasures for little filly Daring Do to find buried on the beach in Horseshoe Bay, hoofmade traps set up outside the house for her to outsmart, and daylong scavenger hunts. The crazy clues Uncle Ad had prepared would force the two of them to spend hours traipsing through the forest. It was messy and glorious.

They'd trot through the squishiest mud and climb up the tallest trees, following a treasure map. When they finally reached the X that marked the spot, they'd found a treasure chest with a set of crowns and their lunch of apple sandwiches and carrot cake inside. *Rulers of the jungle!* they'd chant. *Discoverers of the treasure!* As a result of her uncle's visits, Daring had grown to love all things thrilling. But he was a busy man with important research to do. He would often be called away abruptly, and Daring Do would have to fill the time in between by making her own excitement.

Over the years, she and Uncle Ad had lost touch, but Daring heard through word of muzzle that he was busy hiking through the arctic trails of the Frozen North. Daring recalled their last meeting in a diner just outside Vanhoover a few years back. *It's big, Daring,* he'd said, taking a sip of his hot spiced apple cider. There were dark circles around his eyes, like he hadn't slept in days. *The next treasure I'm going to find is going to change life as we know it. Ponies will never be the same when they hear of this.*

"Your uncle spoke of you often." Thaddeus Vine's scratchy voice pulled her back to the present situation. He crossed over and positioned himself in front of the painting. The ornate golden frame, carved with artistic renderings of at least fifty different flowers, shone under the light of a green glass wall sconce. "Said you were the most fearless pony he'd ever met—even as a filly—but that you were also incredibly stubborn."

Vine delivered a crooked smirk, regarding Daring. "In fact, it was his idea that we throw a banquet just to bait you." His wiry mustache curled up, one side higher than the other.

Daring leaned forward. "You did what?"

"Gallant insisted that you would never *dare* to attend an event you had been formally invited to." Thaddeus walked back over to Daring and added with another chuckle, "That's why we had those ponies trail you and mention it loud enough for you to hear."

The moment came rushing back to Daring. She'd been in the marketplace doing some shopping to stock up on carrots and dandelion tea when she'd heard a couple of mares talking about the banquet. They'd mentioned that it was to include a special presentation of the Botanical Society's findings of new plant species from the past year, and then in hushed whispers they had said the magic words: *Eternal Flower.*

Daring had quickly noted all the details

of the event as muttered by the random ponies and planned to show up the next night decked out in her finest attire, without an invitation. Daring Do didn't need to be invited to things; she just went.

"That sneaky Ad..." It was going to take some adjusting to refer to him by his actual moniker. "I mean, sneaky *Gallant True*." Her uncle's plan had worked.

Daring Do hated being predictable, but it was endearing that her beloved uncle still knew her so well—even after all these years apart. Once she really considered it, she realized that she missed him immensely. Certain innocence returned to her for the briefest of moments—the fleeting feeling of fillyhood.

Daring Do wanted to see her uncle

again as soon as possible, to share with him her stories of triumph in the face of danger. Maybe he would be proud. There had been so many priceless antiquities put safely in museums and powerful relics saved from the wrong hooves. It was a far cry from digging up "buried treasure" in the sand. For one thing, she wasn't so naïve now as to believe that X marked the spot. It never did.

"I'll do it!" Daring announced, puffing up with pride. "I'm going to rescue my uncle, and we are going to find that flower. Anything you can tell me about the specimen that Caballeron nabbed?"

"All we know is that your uncle believed the leaf had been plucked from the stem of the Eternal Flower itself. He said it was the key to all his research—that it would finally allow him to find the bloom with you by his side...." From the way his eyes were becoming watery, it seemed like Vine was more upset about losing the flower than about losing Gallant. Daring thought back to the moment before Caballeron had escaped—Thaddeus had nodded to her. *Let him go.* But why did he want to let him go? It didn't add up.

"He kept saying over and over how he couldn't wait to see you face-to-face," Vine continued. "Those were his words: 'face-to-face.' "

"Well, now that *I'm* on the case, it won't be long until that happens," Daring said as she put her hoof on Vine's shoulder. The touch made him jump. Daring shot him a sideways glance. "Did I startle you?"

"No, of course not!" Thaddeus frowned. "I'm just overwhelmed by the events of the evening, Miss Do. Surely you can understand that." He turned away from her and moved back a few paces. Something about his body language was perplexing.

"I almost forgot!" Willow Fern exclaimed. The old mare hobbled over and procured a tiny object from her clutch. "Gallant wanted you to have this." She gave a weak smile as she passed it to Daring Do.

"A key?" It was made of rusted bronze and shaped like a daffodil, and along one side of its stem, there were several pegs of varying length. Daring Do racked her brain for what it could possibly open. Vine was getting antsy. Willow Fern nodded. "We found it when we searched his office. It had a note attached that—"

Thaddeus cut in. "That *explicitly* stated to give this to you, should anything happen to him." He began to pace around, hooves padding alternately against the wooden floor and the soft red Saddle Arabian rug. "I assume you know what the key unlocks?" He sneered.

"Of course…" Daring lied. She held the key up to the light, turning it over. "It's been ages since I've seen this old thing!" She smoothed her hoof over the worn grooves of the engraved daffodil, buying extra time by appearing deep in thought. In truth, she had no idea what it was for.

But it was a clue, and if there was anything her uncle had taught her, it was that things were not always what they seemed. Daring hid the key inside the secret pocket she'd sewn into her glittering green gown. Pockets were essential in any garment.

Thanks, Uncle Ad, Daring thought. *I love your games and all, but something a little more obvious could help right about now.* The wheels started turning in her head. Daring looked up at the expectant pair and flashed a smile. "Do you mind if I use the library for a few minutes? I need to do some last-minute research."

"Be our guest, dear." Madame Willow Fern grabbed her colleague by his coat lapel and led him out the door. Vine gave Daring a suspicious look, but Willow smiled. "Your uncle always used to say that most of an adventure pony's work takes place inside a library." The door closed behind them, and Daring Do was alone in the reading room.

CHAPTER 5
The Diary and the Everleaf

"Face-to-face, huh?" Daring said to the little key, echoing her uncle's words. "Let's see what we're working with, Uncle Ad." She began to snoop around the room, picking up lamp bases and rattling them, pulling back rugs to check for trapdoors, and pulling the particularly large books off the shelves. Her search yielded nothing, and Daring began to grow frustrated. If only there were some sort of more tangible clue to go on, she might be able to determine where to look. "Face-to-face…" she repeated to herself. Daring's eyes scanned the room once more for a lockbox, a chest, anything that might match the key in her hoof. Whatever it went to surely held more answers!

Suddenly, it dawned on her. *Face-to-face.* Daring rushed over to the portrait of Gallant True and stared into the image of her uncle's face. It was such an accurate likeness—the eyes seemed to tease her for having taken so long to decipher his riddle. There was no doubt that this painting was harboring a hidden message. She squinted, but it only appeared as a blurry version of the bespectacled pony.

Then Daring noticed a small pin on his neck kerchief, a golden arrow that reminded her of the Arrow of Marapore, a recently recovered relic. It was arranged diagonally, with the tip pointed directly at the bottom right corner of the picture. As an experiment, Daring's eyes traced the invisible line all the way to the carved golden frame. There it was—a small opening next to a bundle of Razdonian roses, just big enough for a key. The adventurer smirked.

Sure enough, the daffodil fit perfectly inside. Daring held her breath, twisting the key slowly. There was no telling what she might be about to find. The frame instantly swung open, revealing a secret compartment!

The gold interior echoed the design

of the frame. A single shelf with carvings of flowers all over it bore two items—a worn leather book and a vial like the one Caballeron had stolen. The beautiful leaf inside the vial appeared to be identical as well, displaying every color of green on the spectrum and flecked with gold. Subtle pulsating waves of glittering light surrounded the treasure, reflecting onto Daring's face as she inspected them. There was only one plant this leaf could belong to, but even more questions arose in Daring's mind now that she had it in her possession. Where had Gallant obtained the leaf? Why were there two? Why had Thaddeus Vine been so blasé about letting its sibling get away? And most important—how was it going to help her find the Eternal Flower and rescue her uncle? A small piece of white tape on the bottom of the vial said EVERLEAF 2/2. *So that's what it's called,* Daring thought. Not that the name helped much.

"Maybe there are some answers in here...." The book, though small, felt heavy in her hooves. It could have been her mind playing tricks on her, but valuable items always felt weightier to Daring Do. She looked back over both shoulders to make sure nopony had crept into the library. She half expected Thaddeus Vine to turn up again, but it was still clear. She opened the book.

My Eternal Flower Diary, by Professor Gallant True, it said in her uncle's hoofwriting. Daring Do fumbled to turn the page and read aloud in a low whisper. "'I, Gallant True, have been granted a unique chance to exhume that trophy of the centuries, that living entity of ponykind's mystical desire since the time of Star Swirl the Bearded—the Eternal Flower! I now vow to devote my days, my wealth, and my academic energies to the achievement of this remarkable assignment.'" Her uncle had left his most prized possession in her hooves—his years of research on the Eternal Flower! It was the greatest clue he could have given to her, and it certainly was no mistake.

Daring Do felt a twinge of excitement, just like when she was a filly and the two of them were about to search for treasure together. There was no stopping her now.

She gingerly closed the picture frame compartment, removed the daffodil key, and took one last glance into her uncle's likeness. "Hold tight, Uncle Adventure! I'm on my way."

CHAPTER 6
To Catch a Leaf Thief

Daring soared across the chilly night sky, beating her wings as fast as she could. Low, wispy clouds rushed past, enveloping her body in a cool dewy mist that was refreshing and sent shivers up her spine. Caballeron and his ponies had had a sizable head start on the journey with their easy escape from the banquet and the subsequent briefing in the reading room. Even if Daring was at a disadvantage, she could still revel in how amazing it felt to be out of that ridiculous dress and back in her regular uniform. Her signature olive-green safari shirt and tan pith helmet allowed her to move freely, dodging low branches, forest predators, or whatever other dangerous obstacle might be thrown at her.

Immediately after leaving the Botanical Society, Daring had set out westward toward Smokey Mountain. Her trustworthy instincts told her that Dr. Caballeron and his henchponies wouldn't want to wait long to sell the stolen goods to the highest bidder. If there was to be an exchange of the Everleaf for money, it was definitely going to happen on this very night. The question was—where were the culprits hiding?

"Come out and face me, Caballeron! Don't be the coward I know you are!" Daring shouted down to the bushy treetops. The land below rushed past in a blur of green and black. Nothing yet—no tents or visible campfires in the forest.

The determined Daring Do would not stop until she found the gang of thieves. Gallant's diary had explained one key detail that Caballeron was unaware of—*both* of the Everleaves were needed to locate the flower. This detail was written on the very last page of the diary. Apparently, Gallant had just made the discovery that when the two Everleaves were brought together, they acted like a compass, pointing the way to the flower's exact location. When they were separated, they pointed the other way, away from the flower. Apart, they led the pony astray—in the opposite direction from the seeker's goal.

That wasn't all she'd learned from her uncle's writings. The stallion had left no stone unturned and no book unread in his search for the Eternal Flower. Daring was just grateful she didn't have to start from scratch. Compared to what her uncle had done, the information she'd gathered herself was the tip of the iceberg.

Every page was packed with scratchy hoofwritten notes and drawings done by Gallant himself. Doodles of vines and trees grew through the words as if True had been watering them with his thought process, watching his theory grow and bloom into something tangible.

Each note had also been laboriously categorized: field studies, renderings, theories, location leads. There was one section in particular that seemed especially important. Among the hastily drawn scribbles of various types of flowers and etchings of ancient engravings, there was an elaborate two-page color illustration of what appeared to be plant roots. The top of the page showed the surface of the soil, and the wiry arms of the plant reached down to the bottom.

But something was different about these roots. Instead of continuing to stretch down farther into the ground, each tip curled and folded back into itself, climbing back up toward the surface. The entire effect was an intricate pattern of braided infinity symbols, like organic lace or a delicate piece of jewelry, only the precious pendant was a live flower that provided immortality, not a shiny diamond. Gallant had written along the side: *The Infinity Root—This distinct curved root is the only unchanging element of the Eternal Flower. All other characteristics change each time the flower is seen by pony eyes.*

A flickering light caught Daring's attention. Puffs of black smoke rose up in wavy pillars. A shadowed outline of a pony paced around in front of it. The silhouette was, without a doubt, the villain she had been looking for. The Pegasus bore left, circling back and descending into the thick canopy of forest leaves.

Daring burst onto the scene, wings spread wide and a menacing look on her face. "Hand it over, Caballeron!" She planted her hooves on the cold ground right in front of a henchpony. The stocky stallion had a cropped orange mane and bushy sideburns that traced the line of his strong jaw. He had changed out of his formal outfit from the banquet and was now wearing his usual getup of a brown vest, exposing his cutie mark of a swirl, a star, a sparkle, and a crosshatch on his slate-colored hide. He frowned back at her and scratched his head.

"Rogue!" Caballeron shouted at the confused oaf. "Out of the way! I'll handle this." He sauntered over to Daring, a wicked grin on his face. The dancing flames of the campfire were reflected in his eyes. "Small world, *Daring Do*."

"Not big enough for the both of us, Caballeron." The Pegasus widened her stance, bared her teeth, and let out a low, rumbling growl. "Give. Me. The. Leaf!"

"I'm afraid you're too late...." Caballeron replied, motioning to a silver henchpony with a shaggy mop of a black mane. Even though it was nighttime, he was still wearing dark sunglasses. The pony trotted over, carrying a heavy brown sack that clinked and clanged. The sound of bits. He tossed it to Caballeron, who opened the drawstring, took a look inside, and snickered. "Thank you, Withers." He turned back to Daring, who was still on the defensive. "I already sold it to my best customer: Ahuizotl!"

Daring felt the anger start to bubble up

inside her. What a fool! Now that the leaf was in Ahuizotl's possession, it would be ten times harder to retrieve. And it confirmed one detail that she'd suspected but hoped wasn't true—Ahuizotl, a giant doglike beast and her number one enemy, wanted to find the Eternal Flower. That could only mean one thing. He wanted to become immortal.

"Don't you realize what you've done?" Daring replied, keeping an eye on Caballeron's four henchponies. The way they were lurking around behind him made Daring nervous. Daring knew three of them as Withers, Outlaw, and Rogue, but she didn't recognize the fourth. The new recruit, a light blue Pegasus mare with a slicked-back orange mane and tail, looked especially suspicious. She was a pretty pony with almond-shaped eyes heavily lined in black. Her cutie mark was a white rose with prickly thorns, which implied that she was pure sweetness laced with danger. In other words, the worst kind of mare.

Daring Do took a step closer to Caballeron and narrowed her eyes. "Ahuizotl is going to use that leaf to seek out the Eternal Flower and gain the ultimate prize—immortality! Do you really want that monster to live forever? You're cursing Equestria to an eternity of a beast who terrorizes ponykind for his own personal evil plots!"

"Doesn't really make much difference to me, Do." Caballeron raised a brow. "I plan to spend my days living in luxury thanks to my benefactor. He even paid me extra for hoof-delivering a certain pony of particular use—"

"Where has Ahuizotl taken my uncle?!" Daring roared.

The sky let out a thundering crack, and giant drops of rain began to pour down on them. The campfire went out with a hiss. Withers, Outlaw, and Rogue dived for cover underneath one of the canvas tent awnings, but the light blue Pegasus inched closer, listening to every word of the conversation. Daring shot her a look to stay back. This was not her fight. She avoided Daring's eyes and dropped hers to the ground.

"My, my," Caballeron drawled, brushing

the wet locks of his salt-and-pepper mane back from his thick black eyebrows. "Did somepony just get so worked up that she summoned the Curse of the Pegasus Tzacol? What is that saying again . . . 'Forceful showers bring Eternal Flowers'?" He laughed, looking back to the mare for approval on his humorless joke. "No, no. That would be far too lucky for you, Ms. Do."

"You're ridiculous, Caballeron." Daring Do rolled her eyes. She was now soaked to the hide from the freezing downpour and becoming impatient. At least the wide brim of her helmet had kept her face and mane dry. "And you're wasting my time. I don't care about the flower; I care about going to find my uncle!"

The adventurer took off into the darkness at top speed, letting the rain pelt her. A normal storm she could contend with by bucking her hind legs against any angry cloud in her path, but this was something different. These clouds wouldn't disappear.

There was no other way.

Daring Do spread her wings and flapped them against the gale-force winds. It was a struggle to stay in the air, let alone resist getting tossed about. Her body was heavy from the water, and there were only about ten hooves of visibility in which to navigate where she was even flying. Conditions had never been worse, but Daring Do wasn't afraid. She pushed forward, imagining Gallant's face in her mind.

The sky shook again, and a massive white bolt of lightning hit a tree below, frying its branches and narrowly missing Daring's left wing. She darted out of the way as several more rods shot down from the sky.

"Hey! Wait up!" A muffled voice fought against the noisy clash of thunder.

Daring Do whipped her head around. Caballeron's light blue mare was hot on her tail, struggling against the elements to catch up to Daring. "Back off!"

"I'm trying...to...help you!" she shouted back over the whistling wind, eyes squinting to shut out the torrential rain. "My name is Rosy Thorn!" She picked up her speed, doing a full barrel roll to catch up. *Impressive*, thought Daring. It didn't change anything, though. Daring Do had a strict "no sidekicks" rule. Especially for former cronies of her foes.

"I work alone!" Daring yelled. "Hasn't your boss told you that?"

Rosy caught up to Daring Do. "He's not my boss!"

"It sure looked that way."

"Well, not anymore! I was strapped for cash and he needed extra ponies," Rosy admitted. "It was just a job! But I want to help you!"

"And I'm supposed to trust you now? Please leave me alone!" Daring swerved around, changing her course toward the coast. She remembered something in Gallant True's diary about the Eternal Flower being reported in several instances throughout history growing near large bodies of water. It was unlikely that Ahuizotl would have come to this conclusion himself, but now that he had possession of Gallant True, Daring Do had to consider the gut-wrenching possibility that the information had been pried out of him. What else would the monster want with the aging scholar?

"You have no idea where you're going, do you?" Rosy Thorn shouted. She was still managing to keep pace with Daring Do. The blue Pegasus was right, but Daring was too proud to ever admit that.

"I have a plan," Daring bluffed. She would come up with something once she could shake this bothersome pony.

The misty outline of a mountain came

into view at the same moment the two Pegasi burst through the last rain cloud. The pink-tinged hue of the horizon reached up into the gray sky, signaling the dawn. Once daylight came, Ahuizotl and his ponies would be on the move.

"Go. Away," Daring warned, staring the young Pegasus down. "I'm not going to say it a—"

"But I know where your uncle is!" Rosy blurted out. "I can take you there."

Well, *that* was a different story.

CHAPTER 7

A Fortress on the Edge of the World

"There it is!" Rosy Thorn pulled back the branches of a palm tree to reveal a great temple perched atop a cliff, overlooking the cerulean sea. Vibrant shafts of sunlight broke through the clouds, highlighting the structure in an angelic glow. Gentle waves rhythmically splashed up against the cliff's edge. It would have been an idyllic scene, if it weren't for the sinister activities going on within the temple walls.

The towering building was made of massive stone blocks built into a pyramid. The square base was wider at the bottom, similar to the Fortress of Talacon—the ominous citadel that had crumbled to the ground after Daring Do removed the Rings of Scorchero from the ancient Pillar of Burnination in order to save the region from eight hundred years of unrelenting heat.

"I don't see anypony...." Daring Do leaned forward for a better look, causing the trunk of the tree to sway forward. She squinted through the viewfinder of her trusty binoculars. No movement in any direction. "You're positive this is where Ahuizotl is keeping Gallant True captive?"

"*Absolutely.* I heard him mention it during the exchange of goods back in the forest." Rosy nodded, her brown almond-shaped eyes growing wide with excitement. After the downpour, her orange mane and tail had dried into a frizzy mess instead of their normal sleek style. She smoothed a hoof over them in vain and pointed at a rectangular opening on the perimeter of the temple. "Watch that side door. It's the only one that's open."

It definitely looked like one of Ahuizotl's hideouts, but that didn't explain why or how Rosy Thorn knew where to find it. Daring Do didn't entirely trust her, but so far the blue Pegasus hadn't done anything suspicious. Well, *other* than cavorting with Dr. Caballeron, but that *could* be chalked up to inexperience.

Daring kept one eye on Thorn as she reached inside the secret pocket of her saddlebag. Gallant's diary and the Everleaf were both still there. She gave them a reassuring little pat and looked through the binoculars again. Daring panned over the glittering sea and crystal-clear blue horizon. A couple of gulls were circling the cliffs, squawking. "Well, it *is* near a large body of water, which goes along with what my uncle theorized about the flower's location."

"So...when did he say that?" Rosy inquired. She was trying to hide her curiosity by sounding casual. "Did he say anything else about the Eternal Flower? What it looks like or—"

"What do you care? I thought it was 'just a job'?" Daring raised an eyebrow at the nosy tagalong. *Nice try, Thorn. Like I'm going to reveal all my secrets to a stranger.*

"Oh yeah, it was." Rosy Thorn's smile dropped, and she turned away, retreating into her own thoughts. She spit on her hooves and tried to smooth back her mane again. "I just thought it would be interesting to hear more about this thing that everypony wants so badly. Must be pretty special."

"The only thing you need to know about it is that it's powerful. The Eternal Flower must be destroyed so that it doesn't fall into the wrong hooves…or *claws*, as it were."

Rosy scoffed. "Do you think your uncle would agree with that?"

"Some of it," Daring Do replied. "But that's of little consequence to you."

The two ponies turned back to keeping watch. A few minutes passed.

"Look! Over there! What did I tell you?" Rosy whispered. Her face was written with smug delight. "The place is crawling with Ahuizotl's guards."

Through the viewfinder, Daring could see that the mare was right. Approximately eight ponies wearing feathered hoofcuffs and necklaces filed out the door, carrying weapons and heavy bags. Provisions for an extensive journey, perhaps? The stern gang of stallions trotted down the steps one after another.

A red pony with a white mane called out a command from the front, and the group came to a screeching halt. They turned on their hooves and stood at attention in a straight line facing the door, waiting for their next order, poised with wooden spears at the ready.

They were waiting for somepony, or some*thing.*

Suddenly, Ahuizotl appeared at the door! His furry, dark blue body towered over his pony guards, making the strong stallions look feeble. The beast stretched out one of his sky-blue claws, pointing toward the trees where Daring and Rosy were hiding, though it was obvious that he hadn't spotted the pair. He was too distracted with his own evil plot to notice subtleties in the landscape such as one palm tree that swayed more than the rest.

Flickers of sunlight glinted off his golden zigzag armbands and armored collar. A smile formed on his elongated doglike face and exposed his rows of sharp white teeth. The monster looked down, and the smile grew wider. Ahuizotl was clutching an item in his left claw. Daring Do could guess what it was: *the Everleaf.*

As soon as he unclenched his fist, her suspicions were confirmed. The Everleaf he'd bought from Caballeron—the one that Daring Do and Gallant True needed in order to find the Eternal Flower—was right there in his paw. Ahuizotl pulled the leaf from its vial and laid it flat on a small wooden slab. The green oval spun around in a circle, like the needle on a compass, until its pointed tip faced the direction of the trees, rather than the sea. Ahuizotl said something inaudible, and the ponies all started marching into the jungle.

Ahuizotl picked the leaf back up and waited.

A second wave of henchponies trotted out in formation, each holding a rope that was tied to a pony at the center of the group. Daring Do peered through her binoculars and immediately recognized her uncle, Gallant True. She would know that pony anywhere.

"There he is!" Daring Do exclaimed, momentarily forgetting that he was in need of aid. She was overjoyed to see her uncle. Everything about him was the same as she remembered, except for the deep wrinkles under his eyes. Same old Uncle Adventure, with his cocoa-colored hide, graying yellow hair, and mustache extending up along his jawline. The familiar sight of his cutie mark—a locked treasure chest with two crossed golden keys on the front—brought Daring Do back to her formative years.

Gallant still wore his favorite tan sweater, but one of the leather elbow patches was falling off. It could have been from years of wear and tear, but judging by the soot and dirt covering his whole body, it was more likely from the arduous journey to the fortress and the recent time spent in its grimy dungeons. At least the professor's signature blue scarf folded into his white shirt collar and the glasses on the bridge of his muzzle were intact.

The ponies tugged on the ropes, and Gallant True walked forward, head slumped down, following the procession of thirty ponies and one gigantic blue beast.

"They're moving him to another location," said Daring. Or, more likely, they were moving him *until* they found the location—of the Eternal Flower. Ahuizotl was using him as a personal guide. "The Everleaf is pointing them straight this way. Which means it's wrong, of course."

"I told you he'd be here," Rosy said with a satisfied smirk. "Do you trust me now?"

"No," Daring replied, snatching the

wind of satisfaction from underneath Rosy's wings. "But it's progress." The adventurer didn't have the time nor the patience for petty pats on the back. Rosy deflated.

"So what do we do?" asked Rosy. She spread her blue wings and shifted her body forward, ready to spring off and soar to Gallant's rescue. "I have an idea! Let's soar down and—"

"We wait!" Daring ordered. "You don't go until *I* say to go." Daring Do frowned and stuck her nose right in the pony's face. "Got it, Thorn?" The last thing Daring needed right now was some overeager sidekick messing up an ambush. She'd dealt with that in the past and learned from her mistakes. If Rosy Thorn was going to be a part of this, it was on Daring Do's terms or not at all. It was just the way things had to be.

"All right…" Rosy conceded, folding her wings back into her body. She propped her chin on her right hoof and let out a sigh. "But we should move soon."

"You think I don't know that?" Daring shot her a look. She brought the binoculars back up to her eyes. "Let me see what we're dealing with before we go in blind."

Gallant's hooves were each tied to a rope, and his horn was covered with a Horavian Unichain, a metal cylinder made from interlocking steel chains. So that's why the stallion hadn't been able to use magic to escape! His powers were rendered completely useless while he was wearing the contraption. It was an evil move, even for Ahuizotl. Covering a Unicorn's horn with a Unichain was one of the cruelest, most humiliating punishments known to ponykind. But the beast would stop at nothing to cause trouble, it seemed. Daring shuddered as she imagined a world in which Ahuizotl was immortal. An eternity of chaos and disturbance for ponies everywhere? There was no reality in which she would let that happen.

"They have him wearing a Horavian Unichain. One of these ponies must have the key to it...." Daring Do panned over, searching the rope-wielding red, blue, and orange henchponies. She singled out a particularly large blue stallion wearing more golden adornments than the others. In his left ear, there were four earrings instead of the normal two. Across his eyes was a slash of orange war paint. Definitely a high-ranking henchpony. *"Him."* Daring gestured. "He's the one." Rosy nodded that she understood.

Now all Daring Do and Rosy Thorn had to do was steal the key, retrieve the Everleaf, and rescue Gallant True. All at once. Two Pegasi against a monster and thirty henchponies? No problem at all.

"One more thing, Thorn." Daring held up her hoof.

"Yes, Daring?" Rosy replied, a familiar eagerness in her eyes. It was the same look that Daring wore when faced with danger.

It made Daring feel better about what she was going to say.

"It's every pony for herself out there. If one of us gets captured, there's no going back. Understand?"

CHAPTER 8
The Ambush of Ahuizotl

"On the count of three," Daring announced. She leaned back onto her hind legs in order to get a better launch. "One... two... three!" The two Pegasi burst through the palm fronds, soaring straight toward the mob. They were relying heavily on the element of surprise, which, if used correctly, could give them the upper hoof they needed to distract Ahuizotl. The henchponies weren't the brightest, so they were easy to disorient.

"What is this?!" Ahuizotl roared, spinning around to catch a better look at the intruders. Rosy Thorn flew past him, her right wing an inch from his nose. The monster swatted at her but missed, allowing Daring Do to spiral under his stomach and touch his left foreleg. Ahuizotl felt the tickle of where Daring had brushed him and instinctively dropped the Everleaf to thwack away the pest. "I'll destroy you for this!" the monster snarled in anger. "Any little pony who messes with the great Ahuizotl pays the price!"

The golden Pegasus grinned in triumph and looped back around, intending to snatch up the leaf while Rosy continued to buzz around his head like an angry bumblebee. Ahuizotl leaned back on his hind legs and growled, using both forelegs to try to catch Rosy. But she was fast, swerving in and out of his range like it was a game.

Now on the ground, Daring Do darted left and right, searching for the prize and narrowly avoiding the poisoned arrows that were being shot in her direction by the henchponies on the jungle's edge. The ponies holding Gallant's ropes stood with blank faces, trying to decide whether to drop them and fight, or hold on. They were lost without Ahuizotl's orders. Gallant gave a delighted giggle as he watched his niece in action. "Jolly good show, it is!"

"The leaf, you fools!" Ahuizotl shouted to the rope-holding ponies. "Stop her from getting the leaf!" He pointed to the ground about fifteen trots away. "Over there!"

Three ponies dropped their ropes and galloped over, but it was too late. The Everleaf lay an inch from the stone precipice of the fortress, looming over the churning waves of the sea. Any false moves and the leaf would be taken by the wind down into the water.

Daring Do narrowed her eyes and took off without a second of hesitation. In one continuous motion, she seized the leaf, poked it into a spare glass vial she always had with her, and tossed it inside her saddlebag. "Thanks, Ahuizotl!" Daring smiled. Instead of saving his trinket, he had pointed it out to her. "Saved me the trouble!"

The moment the leaf landed in her bag's secret compartment, the Everleaves gave a massive jolt. "Whoaaaaa!" Daring Do yelled, plummeting to the ground. The shock must have been due to the powerful magical specimens being joined together once again. She felt them begin to shake, and struggled to keep the bag against her side as she pulled herself upright. It would be bad if anypony, especially Ahuizotl, noticed her bizarre behavior—then *both* the Everleaves would be at risk!

"Be careful, Daring!" Gallant called out in concern.

A shriek rang out as Ahuizotl plucked

Rosy Thorn from the air with the claw on the end of his long, skinny tail. "Daring! Catch!" Rosy yelled, and flung a tiny key toward Daring Do. It was for the Unichain! Four henchponies jumped forward to catch it at the same time as Daring, landing on top of the adventurer in a heap of limbs and feathers, some ornamental and some attached to Daring's wings.

Rosy wriggled to free herself from Ahuizotl's grasp, but it only made the beast clench tighter. He cackled in glee.

Meanwhile, over by the doorway, Gallant True grunted as he struggled to fling the last two ropes off his hind hooves, garnering newfound strength from the presence of his niece and her cohort. The old stallion bucked his hind legs against an orange pony, who toppled over like a milk bottle hit by a ball at a county fair game. "Take that, you...insolent hooligan!" He bristled, shaking a hoof at the fallen soldier.

"Don't get up!" Ahuizotl thundered, approaching the pile of ponies. "I want Daring Do trapped under there. She is *mine*." The henchponies did their best to hold their positions, confining the Pegasus in a pseudo-cage built by their bodies.

That was all Daring Do needed to hear. She burst up through the middle, flinging the stallions off her with one hoof in the air, and shot into the sky. "I don't think so!" she called out, a wide smile visible beneath the locks of gray mane that were falling across her eyes. "I belong to nopony, and neither does my uncle!"

At this, Ahuizotl ran for Daring Do, still carrying Rosy in his claw. He reached out, narrowly missing Daring's tail. Rosy freed herself and flew toward her companion, but Ahuizotl managed to grab the blue Pegasus again, a consolation prize for what he had lost. Unfortunately for Rosy, Daring didn't witness her recapture.

"Hurry up, Thorn!" Daring shouted, racing toward Gallant. She scooped him up by the shoulders of his itchy sweater and took off into the sky, wings working twice as hard to carry the extra weight. Once they burst through the cloud cover, Daring slowed for one last glance over her shoulder to check that Rosy Thorn was right behind them. She wasn't. But Daring had told her the deal. Daring Do had a task to complete. And now, with the two Everleaves secured and her uncle by her side, she might actually stand a chance.

CHAPTER 9
The Secret of the Everleaves

They weren't too far away from Ahuizotl's temple, but Daring Do knew that he would never seek them in this direction. The Everleaf had pointed southward, so the beast would reckon that the Eternal Flower was to be found down there. And for all Ahuizotl knew, Daring and Gallant had gone that way as well. The clouds had done an excellent job of hiding their actual course.

"We should be fine to rest here for a moment," Daring assured her uncle, setting him gently down on his four hooves. He touched down on the soft white sand with a heavy sigh of relief. "I was wondering when you'd show up, my *Darling* Do."

"Hey! Don't—" Daring started to protest out of habit. But then she stopped herself—if anypony could call her an old nickname, it was her favorite relative. She stifled a giggle and drew him into an embrace. "I was strategizing!"

"Well, it took you long enough," Gallant replied, removing the Unichain from his horn. "I was getting really tired of pretending to wear that thing."

"Pretending?" Daring's jaw dropped. She held up the hard-won key. "You mean we took the trouble to get this for nothing, and you could have used your magic to help us?" Her mind drifted back to Rosy Thorn and she felt a twinge of guilt. The mare could take care of herself, right? Yes, of course she could.

"I'm afraid so, Poppit." Gallant sat down on the sand and removed his glasses. He unfolded his kerchief and rubbed it on the lenses absentmindedly. "Stole the key myself last night when those dim guards were sleeping. Was wearing the silly thing more for show, you know? You have to let these ponies *think* they are running things. Surely I taught you *that* trick, my dear...."

"Obviously." Daring Do felt like she was five years old, getting quizzed again on tactics. "But let's focus on what is actually important here—you are safe and I have the Everleaves!" She grinned at him, puffing up her chest with pride.

"Yes, yes." True nodded. His horn sparkled with a light blue magic glow, and he placed the glasses back on his muzzle. "I suppose it's a bit better. Not perfect, but it'll do for now."

Daring trotted over to him and looked down. She held up her right hoof. "You're not even going to do the secret congratulatory hoof-bump?"

"Oh, that was for when you were a filly." He laughed. "To keep you motivated. We don't have to bother with it now. You're a grown mare with a successful career of your own!" Gallant stood up and brushed off his sweater, though it made little difference in the ratty garment's appearance. "If you didn't have the leaves, I would be a little surprised. I practically spelled this one out for you, love."

"Thanks." Daring Do rolled her eyes. She must have been delusional to think she'd receive praise from the stallion.

"Fancy a paddle?!" Gallant trotted over to the shore, his yellow mane waving in the wind. He pushed up his wool sleeves and waded out into the refreshing blue water. Daring shook her head with a chuckle. Gallant True was getting even kookier in his old age. She tossed her pith helmet onto the sand but kept her saddlebag on her shoulder. Too many valuables in there to put it down, even for a second.

"So have you studied my diary, then?" Gallant closed his eyes and breathed in the salty air. "Since you found my Everleaf, I take it you found that as well."

"Read it cover to cover," Daring Do assured. She closed her eyes as well. The soft rhythm of the waves made her sleepy. "Is it true that the Eternal Flower changes its appearance after every time it's been seen? And that it replants itself somewhere new?"

"Very good, darling." The old stallion smiled, eyes twinkling with intrigue. "And what else did you learn?" He took a step toward her, intentionally making the water splash up onto her olive-green shirt.

"That the only way to tell the true Eternal Flower is by its vines, which curl up like the symbol of infinity. But I don't understand the Everleaves—where are they from and how do they work?" Daring pressed.

"As for where I obtained them—that must remain a mystery," Gallant said cryptically. He shook off his hooves and trotted back onto the dry shore. "I'm afraid my colleague Thaddeus Vine is the only one who knows that. Shouldn't have told him...but anyhow, let's take a gander at how they work, shall we?"

Daring Do followed him, lifting her bag off her shoulder. She reached inside and unzipped the secret compartment. The two leaves were intact and vibrating like two magnets trying to join each other. After so much hype, Daring Do was eager to see what the Everleaves were capable of.

"Do you remember the three rubrics?"

"The what?" Daring Do tried to recall the information from the diary, but the text was dense and she was going on very little sleep. "Oh, come on, Uncle Ad, can't you just tell me?"

"Very well," Gallant conceded. "If he already knows, you might as well know, too. The diary, please." He held out his hoof.

Daring passed the book over to him, and the pony frantically flipped to a page near the back. From the way Gallant True was acting, Daring Do had clearly glossed over the most important part. "There!"

He pointed his hoof at a little drawing of a stone shield.

"The rubrics were found on an ancient carving at the site of Orshab, the same site where I found the leaves—where legend says that Mooncurve the Cunning took a sip of nectar from the very flower we seek." He showed Daring the image of Mooncurve. He was a tall, thin Unicorn with a long mane, ornamental cuffs on each hoof, and a cloak embroidered with flowers. Daring Do felt like she'd seen him somewhere before. Was it really possible that this pony was still alive somewhere, after thousands of years?

"Rubric number one: 'To read the compass, leaf the pages' ..." Gallant pointed his hoof at the next rule on the page, growing more eager with each passing moment. "Number two: 'To reach the island, travel the scales.'" Gallant began to pace around his niece in a circle. With the soft breeze blowing on the tropical beach, it felt just like the days in Horseshoe Bay. Only this was a real quest, with real stakes. Not a filly's game.

"And number three." Daring finished it off, finally recalling the words. "To reveal the truth, examine the roots."

"Correct!" Her uncle laid the diary down on the sand, opening it to what must have been the only two blank pages in the whole book. He gingerly removed the two Everleaves from their vials, brought them close to his face to inspect them, and then placed them side by side, flat on the parchment. They flew to the pages.

Leaf the pages, Daring thought. *So that's what it meant.* The two leaves began to spin around at a crazy speed.

"They're calibrating to form the compass," Gallant True explained. He kept his eyes on the progress. "It can be on any book, really. But I've only ever tried this one." The leaves stopped, both pointing slightly inward toward each other. "And it works."

"Now what?" Daring said, unimpressed. "That tells us nothing."

"Just wait for it!" Gallant barked. A moment later, two beams of green light shot out from the tip of each leaf, converging into one large beam that pointed straight out to sea. A glowing, visual path to follow.

"There's only one place those leaves

could be pointing." The realization washed over Daring Do like the waves on her hooves. "And it's not the ocean floor." The adventurer reached into her shirt pocket and procured her small lightweight map of the known world. She unfurled it and pointed to a little patch of dots off the western coast. "The Isles of Scaly!"

"Dragon territory…" Gallant breathed in awe, his jaw agape. His glasses slid a few inches down his muzzle. "But of course—*to reach the island, travel the scales*!" He put a hoof on Daring's shoulder. "Nopony can go there, unless they travel by *dragon*. Dragon scales! It makes perfect sense now!" His face suddenly fell. "What are we going to do?!"

"Well, Uncle, I think today's your lucky

day." Daring Do held up a small shell carved with the ancient Symbol of Scaly— a dragon tooth with a five-pointed star in the middle. "I think I know somedragon who can help." She touched the shell to her lips and blew. A sweet whistle rang out, and somewhere in the distance, a scaly green ear perked up.

CHAPTER 10
Travel the Scales

The two ponies gripped the sides of the rope as tight as they could without strangling the dragon. The beast had been kind enough to bow down and let the ponies wrap the rope around his body, understanding that the older one was nervous. Dragons could be intuitive and wise, if they cared to be. Fortunately, this one and Daring Do were old friends. This wasn't the first time Knuckerbocker had saved her hide.

"Stop pulling on the rope so hard!" Daring Do reminded Gallant. She would prefer to fly beside her uncle and the dragon, but the rubrics had clearly stated that they needed to "travel the scales." Besides, the only way any other creature could attempt to enter the realm of the dragons—the Isles of Scaly—was with a host. Ponies had to charm their way to the mystical place if they wanted to visit, though most ponies would never dare. Dragons didn't like intruders.

"Whooaa!" Gallant True called out, looking equal parts terrified and thrilled to be riding on the back of a massive green creature. The beast tilted left, his great wings riding a pocket of warm wind. Gallant slid down, holding on to the rope so tightly his hoof was turning white from the lack of circulation.

Daring stifled a laugh. "And you call yourself an adventure pony?"

"Why do you think I wanted you to come with me, Darling Do?" He lifted his right hoof to pat Daring on the back, forgetting that he was holding on for his life. Daring reached over and grabbed him by the sweater to pull him upright, and he breathed a sigh of relief. "See?!"

"I certainly can't blame you." Daring winked. "*I'd* want to have *me* along on any adventure! But…why didn't you just ask me? Instead of the whole Botanical

Society banquet charade? Wouldn't it have been a lot easier?" Daring smiled and added, "And I wouldn't have had to wear that awful gown."

"After disappearing for all those years?" Gallant asked. It may have been from the wind blowing in his face, but the stallion's eyes looked especially watery. "Would you really have come?"

"No, probably not," Daring admitted, turning her eyes forward. "I was pretty annoyed with you after you stopped writing from the Frozen North. You just disappeared!" Daring Do turned back to him. "But... I'm glad I'm here now."

"Me too, dear." Gallant True breathed a sigh of relief. "Me too."

The golden mare spread her wings

and hugged her uncle. The embrace was stopped short by a hearty growl from Knuckerbocker. The dragon flapped his great wings faster as he began to descend. As they broke through the clouds, it was obvious why. A gorgeous landscape extended out below them, like glistening emerald jewels encrusted on a slab of aquamarine.

They had arrived at the Isles of Scaly.

"How glorious!" Gallant marveled, removing his spectacles. "Each island looks like the curve of a dragon's claw!"

"Five islands total," Daring Do explained. "One for each of the dragon tribes of the sea. Knucker belongs to the largest tribe, which dwells on the biggest island at the top—Octave. That's where we'll start."

Knuckerbocker drew his neck back and let out a stream of fire, signaling his arrival to the realm. Several geysers of fire from various locations around the island shot up in response. He flapped his spiky wings as they touched down into the tropical surroundings, nearby trees swaying from the powerful gusts of wind he was creating.

The dragon's claws made contact with mossy ground. He folded in his wings and leaned down into a deep bow, touching his chin to a patch of teal grass. He expelled a little burst of flames from his nostrils, and the grass instantly burned to a crisp. A second later, the grass regenerated itself, growing in fuller than it was before.

"Fascinating…" Gallant said, eyes growing wide. "The flora is instantly able to restore itself after exposure to fire.…" He pulled a small notepad from his chest pocket and furiously scribbled down a note. "Makes sense for an environment where the primary occupants are dragons." He smiled with sheer delight, his golden mustache glinting in the midday sun. "I can't wait to tell Thaddeus! He'll be so jealous."

"Come on! We have no time for botanical research. There's only one plant we're interested in finding right now." Daring Do slid along the arch of the beast's back, her golden hooves gliding easily along the slippery, iridescent scales. The Pegasus spread her wings, letting them do the rest of the work as she flung her body into the air and landed on the soft soil.

She nodded to her uncle to do the same. His attempt did not go as well, given the lack of wings and general clumsiness of a pony who'd been holed up in a library for the majority of the past few years. "Thank you for the ride, Knucker," Daring said, bowing to the dragon. "One day I will find a way to repay you for your continued aid." It was hard to believe she'd known the dragon for so many years now. Though he'd given her the summoning shell, Daring didn't use it unless there was no other way. This was only the second time she'd invoked its powers.

The beast closed his enormous azure eyes and nodded that he understood.

A second later, Knuckerbocker took off again, vanishing into the sky. His green outline dissolved into the misty atmosphere. At the same time, two purple dragons drew closer. They looked like they were going to land on a different island.

"Amazing creatures, dragons," Gallant True marveled, shielding his eyes as he watched the pair soar across the sky. "And so fortunate that you know one so we could come here, Daring! What a wild adventure! The Eternal Flower is within our reach."

Daring Do turned around, surveying the dense foliage with focused intent. The sweet scent of blooms and freshwater attacked her senses. Every direction was a blossoming oasis filled with a hundred different shades of green, punctuated by bright bursts of exotic color. The trill of insects filled the air, and the warm sunlight permeated the growth in small, glowing patches. Daring Do took a step forward and accidentally put her hoof down right on a group of Dindiwigs. The little red bugs crawled up, pincers poised. Daring stomped her hoof down again, and they all went flying off. "Argh!" she grunted in frustration. "Can you please do the thing with the leaves so we know where we're headed at least?"

"Oh yes. Of course!" Gallant True brought out the Everleaves and placed them on the diary again. They began to spin, just as they had before. When they stopped, they tilted into each other, projecting the green beams of light in the direction of a small clearing. "Straight ahead to the Eternal Flower!" Gallant chirped, trotting toward the path. When his niece didn't follow, he stopped and called out, "Aren't you coming, Daring?"

But Daring Do didn't reply.

Instead, a familiar voice called out, "Just lead the way, Professor...."

Gallant True whipped around to find himself face-to-face with Ahuizotl! The monster was grinning wickedly, holding Gallant's beloved niece hostage in his big tail claw. There were two hench-ponies by his side, lugging his wares, and another pair lurking in the shadows behind them.

"Surprised to see us, Mr. True?" Ahuizotl

cackled. "You aren't the only one who knows how to be persuasive with dragons, it seems. Surrender yourself now or be taken by force!"

The beast wasn't alone. "You'd better listen to him, Gallant…" said Mr. Thaddeus Vine, walking into the light, "…or suffer the consequences." His pale green complexion and cutie mark of a curled ivy vine seemed to fit into the lush environment perfectly. Since Daring Do had only seen him in his formal suit at the banquet, the pony's tan utility shirt looked odd, especially since he still wore his monocle along with it.

"Thad?" Gallant's face fell. "What in Star Swirl's name are you doing?"

"I'm taking what belongs to me."

"Release me!" Daring demanded. Vine watched the Pegasus struggle to free herself from Ahuizotl's grasp. Vine sighed. "This will all be much easier if you two just cooperate."

"Never!" Daring shouted back. "I'd rather suffer the wrath of the Ketztwctl Empress's dark enchantments than help you for one second!"

"I told you she'd say that," said a sweet voice from the shadows. "Maybe I can convince them to help us. After all, we're old friends...."

"Good idea." Vine motioned to somepony behind him. "I do believe you've met my sister, Miss Rosy Thorn." The blue Pegasus stepped forward, looking prim and put together. Her dirty old vest had been abandoned for a shiny gold blouse, and her orange mane and tail were slicked back, smooth and sleek. A ridiculous outfit for a journey into the unknown, thus proving that Rosy was a total amateur.

"Nice to see you again, Gallant." Rosy batted her blackened eyelashes with practiced perfection. "Though I don't think we've been formally introduced. The last time we graced each other's presence was when you and your selfish niece were *abandoning* me after I helped you escape. Not very nice…"

"Hey!" Daring thrashed her body against Ahuizotl's grip. "We said it was everypony for herself!" It was one thing to be a traitor, but to be a revisionist as well? Despicable.

Gallant loosened the blue scarf around

his neck. He looked crestfallen. "I…
uh…" He stared at Thaddeus Vine, trying
to read him, to understand his motives.
How could his own colleague, *his friend*,
have betrayed him like this? He puffed
up and shouted out in an uncharacteristic
fit of rage, "Vine, you filthy conspirator!
Do our years of careful research mean
nothing to you?! Think of the Eternal
Flower!"

"On the contrary, my dear colleague,"
Vine replied. "They mean *everything* to me.
And to my top benefactor here, Ahuizotl,
as well. That's why you and your 'darling'
niece are going to take us to it. We plan to
see if your theories really do hold up, since
you would never share all your research
with me before." Vine smirked and raised

a brow. His monocle moved with it. "Now's your big chance to be right, Gallant."

Thaddeus Vine might as well have just uttered a magic spell. If there was anything Daring Do's uncle loved in this world, it was being proven correct.

CHAPTER 11
An Oasis of Fire and Flowers

The beams of green light continued to highlight the way, growing brighter as they drew closer to the location of the Eternal Flower. The motley crew soldiered on with Daring Do and Gallant True at the helm, followed by the two henchponies pointing spears at their flanks. Then it was Vine, Rosy, and Ahuizotl at the rear.

The island landscape was a beautiful revolving display of palms, grassy patches rimmed in wildflowers, and rocky cliffs looking out onto the choppy waters and purple-sand beaches. If they weren't being held hostage, Daring Do might have actually enjoyed it.

But there were still so many unseen dangers to be wary of that Daring secretly wondered if any of her captors had bothered to do their research on the Isles of Scaly. Her guess was no, considering none of the ponies seemed too concerned about the possibility of poisonous insects, sinkholes, or acid rain showers, in addition to the dragons lurking everywhere.

Daring Do crept across the island, taking great pains not to disrupt anything.

Each hoofstep was mindful. But it was all in vain, as the sound of Vine's clunky hooves against the ground behind her was the opposite of stealth. Combined with Ahuizotl's clambering through the trees, touching every plant in his path, they were sure to draw some unwanted attention.

A random blast of fire shot up into the sky in the distance, and Ahuizotl tried to hide his fearful shivers. What a coward Daring's nemesis truly was, to be afraid of dragons! When Daring considered it, it made sense to her. The biggest bullies were usually the ones who were secretly afraid of everything.

Gallant True stopped in his tracks.

"Keep going, old stallion," Thaddeus

shouted in amusement. "You're not finished yet."

"I would, Thad, but it seems we are at an impasse." Gallant stared down through his glasses at the edge of the land and the mouth of a wide, bubbling river. The green beam of Everleaf light shone straight toward it. "Any ideas? Thaddeus, since you're so brilliant, maybe you have something to say...."

"Well, clearly we need a raft of some sort," Vine announced. "Not all of us are Pegasi."

"Henchponies!" Ahuizotl thundered. "Build us a raft!" The two stallions panicked, scrambling to gather loose branches from the surrounding area. Ahuizotl laughed as he watched them construct a crude vessel.

"Hurry up! I can feel the Eternal Flower getting closer...." Ahuizotl proclaimed, looking out to the river. "Soon I will be the only creature in all of Equestria who will LIVE FOREVER!" The beast pointed at Gallant True and Daring Do. "And you, Daring Do, are going to help me achieve this feat!"

"Oh, *Ahuizotl*..." Daring Do hung her head in mock concern and began to shake it back and forth. "You don't know a single thing about the Eternal Flower...do you? What does it even look like?"

"Don't insult me, Do!" Ahuizotl roared. "It's the most beautiful flower the world has ever known. I will know it when I see it...."

Daring was careful to keep one eye on the double-crossing, slick-haired liar

Rosy Thorn and the other on her brother. Daring Do had never really quite trusted Vine. Even back in the reading room at the Botanical Society, the pale green stallion had been a nervous wreck—nothing but shifty eyes and pacing around. Now Daring knew why. She supposed it would be quite difficult to act natural around a pony you were planning to betray later on.

Thaddeus had given Daring a sly nod in the ballroom, one that implied she should let Dr. Caballeron escape with the Everleaf. It had all been part of the grand plan to intrigue Daring Do, have her secure the missing items via the daffodil key, retrieve the other Everleaf, and finally join forces with Gallant True to figure things out. Daring's fearlessness and cunning paired with Gallant True's expertise on the Eternal Flower made them the only duo who could solve the mystery. In some ways, Thaddeus Vine should have been applauded for his foresight into the way the events were going to unfold.

But there was no way Daring Do was going to let this journey end the way Vine and Ahuizotl wanted it to. She had to take action now.

CHAPTER 12
Indigenous Plants and Ingenious Plans

"Pssst! Gallant!" Daring tried to catch Gallant's attention. Now that the henchponies were occupied with building the raft, the two of them could easily escape. Daring readied herself to carry the weight of her uncle again. If it meant flying to another island while holding Gallant True by his wool sweater, then so be it. First, though, she'd have to snatch the Everleaves back, which would be trickier. Vine had them in his hoof, set on top of the blank pages that Gallant had cleverly ripped from the diary in order to keep it safe.

"Uncle Ad!" Daring tried again. But Gallant True was far too busy crouching down, inspecting an indigenous plant to notice that Daring was trying to hatch an escape plan. The brown pony was lighting a fern on fire with a match, watching it burn, then laughing with delight as it grew back instantly each time. It was just like the grass that Knuckerbocker had burned with his fire breath after landing on the island. Gallant bent down and scooped up a few pieces of the fern, roots and all, and put them inside his pocket. Daring rolled her eyes. She'd grab him when the time came.

"If you're thinking about escaping— don't." Rosy flew over to her and landed uncomfortably close. "You've seen me in action. I'm fast enough to catch you."

Daring narrowed her eyes. "What's in this for you, anyway, Thorn?" Daring should have listened to her first instinct back at Caballeron's encampment: the one that had told her to stay far away from this mare.

"It's like I told you." Rosy shrugged with a wicked smirk. "It's a job."

"What? Couldn't get anypony else to hire you?" Daring Do teased. "Had to get your big bad brother Thaddeus to pull a favor?" Daring adjusted her pith helmet and brushed a black lock of mane away from her dirty face. The contrast between Daring Do and the elegant Rosy Thorn had never been more obvious.

"On the contrary...I recruited Rosy because I knew she'd be perfect," Vine interjected. Daring spun around to face him. She could tell he was savoring this explanation. Vine was incredibly proud of himself and wanted kudos for setting it all up.

"You see," he continued, circling around the two mares, "I needed somepony who could play the part with both Caballeron and you. He's stupid enough not to notice an interloper. But not just anypony could trick you, Daring. I *do* have to give you credit for that much." Vine smiled and put a hoof on Rosy's delicate shoulder. "Rosy here is an excellent actress. Don't you agree, Do?"

"Vine," Daring replied, "I think your whole family is excellent at deception and lies. Maybe you should all start a theater company!"

Over by the water's edge, the two henchponies grunted and moaned as they tied the last section of wood together. Drops of sweat were rolling down their faces. "Fix it now!" Ahuizotl growled in a fit of rage. "Or I'll make a raft out of you!" The blue one hopped onto the structure to test its strength, and several pieces of wood dislodged, carried away by the strong current.

"Looks structurally sound, boys," Gallant

teased. "Mind if I have a go?" He began to shoot blasts of green magic from his horn at a nearby pile of sticks and jungle vines. They floated over, arranging themselves into a perfect grid. More blasts of magic tied the vines around them. Gallant repeated the steps a few times until it looked secure. "I've still got it!" The old stallion grinned, stepping onto his own stable watercraft. It was just big enough for two—him and Daring Do. He trotted back and forth, inspecting the double hoofrail.

The henchponies watched, mouths agape.

Out of nowhere, an explosion of flames burst forth, narrowly missing the rafts. "RAAAAAAAAAAAAAAWR!" an angry dragon roared, diving down toward the ponies and chomping its massive

sharp-toothed jaw. Every plant in the vicin-
ity swayed back and forth from the high
winds caused by the beast's wings. The
gusts were so powerful that they knocked
the ponies right off their hooves. Even
Ahuizotl came crashing to the ground,
limbs flailing.

The scaly crimson brute flew around
the fallen travelers, shooting fire at them.
He flew up into the sky momentarily and
came nose-diving back down again. There
was one peculiar thing about the dragon's
behavior, though. Daring and Gallant
must have realized it at the same moment.

"He won't go near the river!" Daring Do
shouted to her uncle. "He's afraid of it!"

"Onto the boat!" Gallant True ordered.
He reached his hoof out to her. "Quickly!"

"Just need to grab two things first!"

The golden Pegasus darted underneath the wing of the dragon, heading straight for Vine, who was fighting to pull himself up from the ground. The dragon roared again, causing Vine to turn his head away. It was just enough time for Daring Do to snatch the Everleaves from underneath his hoof and take off again.

"Good luck finding the flower now!" Daring shouted. "Or ever getting off this island!" Now, with her prize secured and her enemies disarmed, Daring Do hopped onto her uncle's raft.

CHAPTER 13
Tears of the Dragon

The two adventurers barreled down the river at top speed, rushing toward the unknown. The tiny yet sturdy raft thrashed back and forth on the gurgling water. Drops of moisture obscured the view from Daring Do's binoculars, making it difficult to survey the landscape ahead for possible obstacles while stopping every three seconds to wipe them clean on the hem of her shirt. Gallant True was lying on the raft, struggling to align the Everleaves guiding light compass and steady himself at the same time, lest he be unceremoniously thrown overboard.

"Aha!" he finally shouted over the commotion. "Show us the way!" The green beam pointed straight ahead, parallel to the river and into the deep uncharted territories of the Isles of Scaly. The scenery on either side was becoming denser with trees, and the sky was starting to turn the pink hue of sunset. The scent of blossoms wafted through the air, taunting the two ponies with the notion that they might actually find the elusive flower any moment.

"We're almost there." Gallant True looked over his shoulder, pulling himself against the hoofrail. He trotted to the back of the raft and let out a heavy sigh. "I still can't believe Thaddeus would betray me like that," he muttered under his breath. "But it wouldn't be the first time that the search for the Eternal Flower has turned somepony into a monster, I would think." He wondered where the mischievous group was now. There was no sign of the rickety raft in the distance. "Do you think we lost them, Daring?"

"For now," Daring replied with a nod. She held her binoculars up to scan the sky for dragons. "But knowing how determined Ahuizotl is to find the Eternal Flower, we're not safe yet." She trotted to

163

the front of the raft to survey the area. "Does it seem like the river is becoming narrower to you?" Daring pointed to each side of the raft. "We are closer to shore on both sides, I'm positive."

"I agree." Gallant nodded and stood up. "We must be close." The waters were starting to calm. Up ahead, the river split into two streams. The green beam of light became brighter, pointing them to the right of the fork.

Daring Do steered the raft using a stick as an oar. The duo soon found themselves in a quiet little cove. The sounds of the squawking birds and roaring dragons had ceased. The only noise was that of a bubbling waterfall. Daring gasped when she saw it.

It wasn't just any waterfall; it was an

enormous ancient carving! The stone cliff had been whittled down to mimic the menacing skull of a dragon. Jagged stone teeth jutted out from the roof of its mouth like stalactites, with the bottom hinge of the dragon's jaw submerged under the water. Steady streams of water fell from its hollow eyes as if the great reptile was crying and the river had been created from centuries of dragon tears. A shiver went up Daring Do's spine, and she knew they were on the right track. Treasure usually lurked in the spookiest places.

"I think we have to enter through its mouth." Daring Do gestured to the spiky archway. "Under the waterfall."

Ahuizotl's cackle suddenly echoed across the cove, sending another shiver up her spine. "After you, Daring Do!"

CHAPTER 14
Grotto of the Moon

"Stay back, Ahuizotl!" Daring Do hollered as she steered the raft into the mouth of the stone dragon. She cursed herself for not moving fast enough to lose Vine and the others. How had they managed it? Perhaps Thaddeus had paid attention to Gallant's magic from before and copied his raft construction. The stallion was known for stealing his colleague's ideas after all.

"Get ready," Daring warned her uncle. The waterfall rained down on the ponies, drenching their bodies from head to hoof, but Daring hardly had time to react. Within a moment of pushing through to the other side, she was magically dry again. She and Gallant exchanged a surprised look.

"What is this glorious place?" Rosy Thorn whispered in awe as the other raft came through and she took in the scene. "It doesn't even seem real!" And for once, Daring Do had to agree with her.

They were now floating in an incredibly beautiful crescent-shaped grotto. Every inch of every visible surface was covered in a spectrum of vibrant flowers of all shapes and sizes, soft dewy moss, and long-armed ferns reaching out to welcome them. The sweet air alone was overwhelming—delicious-smelling perfumes battled one another for the prize of sweetest. Fireflies danced lazily about, lighting up the dusky dark with their magic.

"I know exactly where we are." Gallant closed his eyes with a smile, inhaling the fresh air. "The Grotto of the Moon." He gestured to their surroundings, unable to contain his excitement. "We made it! The Eternal Flower is here."

Everypony looked around in a panic, hoping to be the one to find the bloom first. "Get out of my way!" Ahuizotl leaped onto the shore, crushing several ferns in the process. He looked left and right, then turned back around and barked at his servants, "Don't just sit there! Find me the Eternal Flower!"

The henchponies snapped to action, leaping onto the other side. They began frantically trotting along the perimeter with their muzzles about an inch from the foliage. A red stallion stopped to inspect a large yellow bloom with a pink center. After a single sniff, he stood back up, swayed for a moment, and then fell flat on his face.

"Somnambular Bloom," Gallant said with a shrug, still mesmerized by his surroundings. He took off his glasses, and his smile grew even larger. He whispered to himself, "Just amazing…"

"Okay, Uncle. We need to focus. What

are we looking for?" Daring whispered, watching Ahuizotl scramble around the grotto, gravitating to each fancy-looking flower he saw—which was practically all of them.

Ahuizotl furrowed his brow in confusion. "We have to find this thing before they do!"

Rosy flew to the top of a large rock for a better view of the grotto. Vine fumbled to exit the raft, but his weight overwhelmed it, and he went splashing into the teal water. He clambered to the mossy ground and pulled himself up, dripping wet. It was a matter of seconds before he was dry again. He raced toward a purple flower edged in white starbursts.

Gallant seemed so calm, despite the craziness unfolding around him. "Patience, darling," True advised coolly. He leaned in and whispered into her ear. "There's no way to know what the flower looks like. It must reveal itself to us when it's ready. Remember the rubrics?"

Daring thought back to their conversation on the beach. So far, the other two rules had come true—the Everleaves had acted as their compass, and they'd arrived on the island by way of dragon scales. "Do you mean"—Daring turned to her uncle—" 'to reveal the truth, examine the roots'?"

The Pegasus had no idea if Gallant responded because she was instantly sucked below the surface of the water by some invisible force. And there was no way up again.

CHAPTER 15
The Infinity Root

She had expected to find herself underwater, paddling to get back to the surface, so Daring Do was shocked to discover that she was in some sort of other dimension. A topsy-turvy pocket below the grotto. The Pegasus marveled at the peculiar sight of it. For instead of the blooms of the gorgeous flowers of the grotto above, this side was a sprawling landscape of upside-down plants. The roots were growing up from the ground in spiky, clawlike formations, extending into the invisible dirt.

It was as if the entire grotto had been flipped over.

Daring Do looked at the ground. Her hooves were solid on the surface of the water, like it was a wavy glass window. Daring Do could see the bottom of her uncle's raft and the land surrounding the pool. Daring trotted over to the land and found Ahuizotl and Vine scrambling around the flower beds. She followed the action, hoping that they wouldn't discover anything while she was stuck in this nothing place.

What exactly was she doing down here? Then Daring remembered that right before she had been sucked down, she had spoken the last rubric aloud. That was it! Daring Do needed to "examine the roots"!

As Daring walked along inspecting the various roots, she began to feel hopeless. The garden of vines provided little variation from one another. But when Daring Do finally saw it, the illustration from her uncle's diary flashed into her mind. Curved, a pattern of lace, the symbol of forever—the roots of the Eternal Flower itself. "The Infinity Root!"

The pony approached the specimen in awe, noting that though the roots were quite spectacular, the flower attached to it on the other side was quite ordinary. A modest white bloom with five white petals, situated between an indigo hibiscus and a fuchsia rose that was the size of Daring's helmet. It was a single plain Jane among a mass of showstoppers.

Daring Do felt a jolt, and her body lurched forward. She came up, gasping for air. The fragrance of the grotto hit her nostrils again, and she knew that she was back. It was as if nopony had noticed her absence at all! Not even Gallant True, who was still waiting patiently for some mysterious event to occur.

"Gallant! I've seen it! *I know*," Daring hissed. She quickly glanced around to make sure nopony was listening in. "I know which one is the Eternal Flower."

"How?" Gallant replied, grabbing her shoulder with his hoof. "Did it happen? Did you see the roots? I knew it!"

"At long last, I've found it!" Ahuizotl bellowed, leaning down to a patch of blossoms. "Now I will experience the glory of everlasting life!" He threw his head back and let out a deep, victorious laugh. When Daring Do saw where he was standing, her heart skipped a beat. He was right next to the Eternal Flower! Had he miraculously figured it out as well? Or was it just a lucky guess?

"Prepare to bear witness to this historical event!" Ahuizotl announced. "Watch closely, *Daring Do.*" Rosy Thorn and Thaddeus Vine hung nearby, watching in bewilderment. Daring readied herself to pounce, just in case he actually chose the right one.

With a flourish, the beast reached down and touched the indigo hibiscus to his lips. And then the formidable Ahuizotl shrank down to the size of mouse. "NOO-OOOoooooo!" he called out in defeat, the richness of his voice shrinking along with him until it was not much more than a tiny squeak.

Thaddeus Vine laughed in triumph and leaned down to the minimonster. "How silly of you, Ahuizotl. Do you not know a Poison Joke Flower when you see one?!"

Ahuizotl responded with a series of angry squeaks, shaking his tiny fist at Vine. The two terrified henchponies, who were now both awake, trotted over and scooped up their leader. They ran back to the raft and headed toward the waterfall, looking back at the grotto as if it were about to eat them up.

"Guess it's just us against you now, Vine." Daring sneered. She leaped onto a nearby rock, maintaining high ground right above the flower. "And something tells me that you have no idea what you're doing."

"Wrong again, Daring." Thaddeus's mustache curled up at the ends, forming a mischievous expression. "I know that one of these two flowers here is the one." He gestured to the fuchsia rose and the white flower.

Daring Do didn't let the fact that he was right register on her face. "What makes you think that?"

"Because I watched you two as Ahuizotl made his selection." Vine raised his eyebrows. "There's no way you would have gotten nervous if he hadn't been close...."

Thaddeus hunkered down on his hind legs and leaned into the rose. He inhaled deeply, yanked the flower from the ground, and drank from the center.

For a moment, it seemed that the pony was unaffected by the bloom. Gallant True winked at Daring. *Be patient*, he mouthed. *Watch.*

"Thad!" Rosy Thorn screamed, her pretty face contorting in horror. "What's happening to you?" Her brother's face was beginning to puff up like a balloon. His cheeks expanded, his eyes bulged, and his monocle popped out. Thaddeus floated up into the air, another victim of the grotto.

Rosy spread her wings and took off after him. The blue Pegasus looped her arm around him, and the two disappeared into the orange sunset, a diminishing blur of blue and green on a cloudless sky.

"Tsk, tsk." Gallant True shook his head as he watched them fly away. "I'm surprised dear Thaddeus didn't recognize that as a Southern Swelling Rose. Never did study enough, that pony. Always cutting corners with his research."

"I think he'll always remember it now!" Daring chuckled, taking a place by his side. She nudged her uncle. "Shall we?"

Gallant True nodded. He and Daring Do gingerly stepped forward and approached the Eternal Flower from either side. This was the moment they had been waiting for. The old professor's eyes filled with tears of joy as he knelt down. He caressed the flower with his hoof. The petals sparkled, lit by the young moon and the reflection of the fireflies.

"Aren't you going to collect it?" Daring Do asked her uncle.

"It was wonderful to see," said Gallant True. He stood up, brushed off his sweater, and cleared his throat. "But let's go home, Darling Do."

CHAPTER 16
The Treasure

The plump Unicorn waitress magically set down two steaming plates of corned carrot hash and potatoes in front of the old professor and his niece. "Can I get you ponies anything else?" she asked with a flip of her curly brown mane. The mare's cutie mark was a set of salt and pepper shakers, and her smile was warm. "More cider for you, sir?"

"Yes, please!" Gallant True held up his empty stein. "Thanks, Pepper Mill!"

"You got it," she replied with a wink, and sashayed off to the kitchen. It was nice to be seated at a cozy pub in Horseshoe Bay enjoying a hard-earned meal. It had been a long journey back from the Isles of Scaly.

"There's one thing I still don't understand, Uncle Ad." Daring Do took a big bite of hash and continued speaking with her mouth full. "Why didn't you want to bring the Eternal Flower back with you to Equestria?"

"It's a funny thing, Daring." Gallant looked down at her through his glasses, which meant he was being serious. "Sometimes you spend a lifetime chasing something, then when you get it, you find out that it was really the chase you loved all the while."

Daring breathed a sigh of relief. "So you never wanted to become immortal?"

"Heavens, no!" Gallant laughed through a large bite of food. "Nopony or *beast* should live forever, my dear. What an awful curse to have upon one's head!"

Daring Do shook her head and frowned in confusion. "But even if you didn't want immortality, I thought you wanted to study the Eternal Flower's magical properties." She lifted her cider stein to her mouth. "Why did you leave it? You even destroyed the Everleaves and your diary! Now you can never find it again."

"After seeing the way Thaddeus and Ahuizotl acted, I realized it was too dangerous to be found," Gallant explained.

"It pains me to say this where a priceless treasure is concerned," Daring said, lifting her cider into the air in salute, "but I think you made the right decision."

"I know." He smirked and leaned in. "Besides, I've found something much better to study: regenerative plants! Remember, on the island, how the plants had evolved to grow back after being burned in order to coexist with the dragons? I saved samples and will study them and figure out how they do it. It's so thrilling! And it's going to make me a hero of the Botanical Society, possibly even a hero of Equestria. I think I am going to call them

Phoenix Flora. Maybe I could publish a paper on it in *Flora and Foalna*...."

And so, with the secret location of the Eternal Flower once again secure, ponykind was saved from its unwitting curse, thanks to Daring Do!

THE END

A. K. Yearling's adventure novels starring the fearless Daring Do have been recognized as the bestselling series in Equestrian history. Yearling holds a degree in literature from Pranceton University. After college, she briefly worked as a researcher at the National Archives for Equestrian Artifacts and Ponthropology in Canterlot. During that time, she wrote an essay based on her findings of the griffon territories, entitled "What Was the Name of That Griffon Again? Or, Beak and Roaming Studies Recalled." It was published by the University of Equexeter's journal, *Pegasus*, last year. She enjoys quiet time alone at home and long trots on the beach.

G. M. Berrow loves to explore exotic locales around the globe, through both the stories she writes and her escapades in real life. Berrow is overjoyed to have collaborated on these adventures with her very own golden idol—A. K. Yearling herself! She adores shiny things, but she thinks the best treasure of all is a book.

GLOSSARY

Ahuizotl (Ow-whee-ZOH-tul): A giant, evil beast who will stop at nothing to gain riches and power. He is Daring Do's biggest foe.

Curse of the Pegasus Tzacol (ZAH-cohl): An ancient myth that foretells of a great storm, brought on by the actions of a curious Pegasus named Tzacol, who entered a sacred weather temple when he was forbidden to do so. He later became a protector of the sky.

Dr. Caballeron (Cab-uh-LAIR-on): A rival treasure-hunting pony. Ever since Daring Do refused to work with him as partners, he's made his bits by doing Ahuizotl's dirty work.

Equestrian Botanical Society: An exclusive club for botanists and environmental science scholars in the land of Equestria.

Eternal Flower: A magical flower believed to grant whoever drinks its nectar immortal life. It changes its physical appearance each time it is found, rendering it extremely difficult to locate and recognize.

Everleaf: A preserved leaf specimen plucked from the Eternal Flower. Gallant True theorizes that the two leaves together will lead to the current location of the flower.

Flora and Foalna: A monthly scholarly journal of the Equestrian Botanical Society.

Gallant True: Daring Do's uncle, fellow thrill seeker, and plant scholar, whom she affectionately refers to as Uncle Adventure. Gallant True spent years exploring the Frozen North, researching plants and searching for clues about the Eternal Flower.

Grotto of the Moon: An oasis found behind a waterfall on Octave, one of the Isles of Scaly.

Infinity Root: A distinct, curved root that is the only unchanging element of the legendary Eternal Flower. All other characteristics of the bloom change each time the flower is seen by pony eyes, rendering it nearly impossible to find.

Isles of Scaly: A group of five islands. Each is shaped like a dragon's claw and is home to a separate tribe of dragons.

Knuckerbocker (NUK-ur-bok-ur): The Octavian dragon that Daring Do once saved from an imprisonment enchantment. Forever in her debt, he then aided in the recovery of the Radiant Shield of Razdon and gifted Daring with a relic of Scaly—a summoning shell to use whenever she needs assistance.

Madame Willow Fern: A member of the board of the Equestrian Botanical Society. One of the foremost experts on unique flora and saplings. Three-time nominee and two-time winner of the Botanist of the Year award, primarily for her work with Wakeful Blossoms.

Octave (AHK-tayve): The largest island and dragon tribe in the Isles of Scaly, and home to Knuckerbocker.

Rosy Thorn: A freelance adventure Pegasus hired by Dr. Caballeron to assist in missions and raids.

Rubrics: Three clues that could lead to the location of the Eternal Flower. They were discovered by Gallant True on an ancient carving at the site of Orshab, the same site as the Everleaves. (Legend says that Mooncurve the Cunning took a sip of nectar from the Eternal Flower there.)

Somnambular (Som-NAM-bew-ler) Bloom: Large tropical flowers with fuchsia petals and orange stems. These dangerous blooms are known to lull ponies to sleep with their strong perfume, though some varieties affect the pony by making him or her sleepwalk. Commonly found in the southern regions and several tropical isles off the western coast of Equestria.

Symbol of Scaly: The symbol of the dragon tribes that dwell on the Isles of Scaly—a dragon tooth with a five-pointed star in the middle.

Thaddeus Vine: A member of the board of the Equestrian Botanical Society specializing in ivy and grasses, with a special interest in magic blooms.